He is not too big.
LITTLE IS BEST!

Yes, he can!

Can Danny get the ball?

Little Danny tries.

Not Mother and Father!

They are too big.

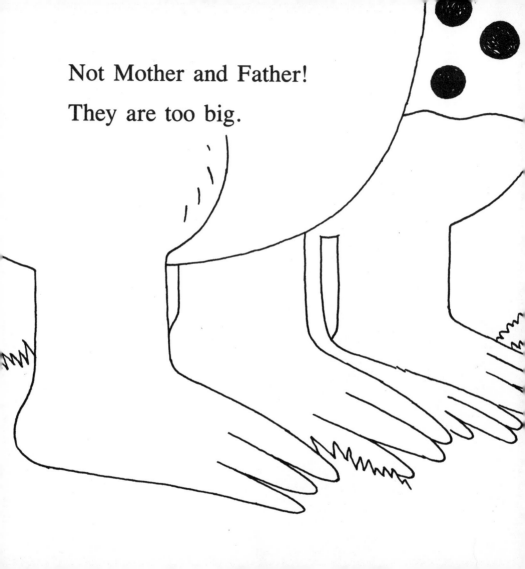

Not Sister! Not Brother!
They are too big.

Who can get the ball?

There! There is the ball.

Where is the ball?

Can Father hit the ball far?

Yes, he hits the ball *very* far!

He hits the ball *too* far.

Can Danny hit the ball far?

No, he can not.

Mother hits the ball far.

Sister hits the ball far.

Brother hits the ball far.

One day, Sister says,

"Who can play ball?"

Little Danny tries and tries.

But Danny is not strong.

Is Danny strong? No!

Mother and Father are very,
very strong.

Brother is strong. Sister is strong.

Little Danny

wants to be strong.

Is Danny loud? No!

No matter how he tries,

Danny is not loud.

"*ROAR,*" says Sister.

"*ROAR,*" say Mother and Father.

Little Danny
wants to be loud.

"*ROAR*," says Brother.

No matter how he tries,

Danny is not big.

Is Danny big? No!

Mother and Father are *very* big.

Brother is big.

Sister is big.

Little Danny wants to be big.

Library of Congress Cataloging in Publication Data

———
    Little Danny Dinosaur.

    (A First-start easy reader)
    Summary: Smaller than the rest of his family, Danny
tries hard to be big and strong—until one day his size
proves to be just right.
    [1. Size—Fiction.   2. Dinosaurs—Fiction]
I. Harvey, Paul, 1926-   ill.   II. Title.   III. Series.
PZ7.P1762Lj   1988   [E]   87-16228
ISBN 0-8167-1229-8 (lib. bdg.)
ISBN 0-8167-1230-1 (pbk.)

Little Danny Dinosaur

Written by Janet Craig

Illustrated by Paul Harvey

Troll Associates

A First-Start Easy Reader

This easy reader contains only 43 different words,
repeated often to help the young reader develop
word recognition and interest in reading.

Basic word list for *Little Danny Dinosaur*

and	hit	says
are	hits	sister
ball	how	strong
be	is	the
best	little	there
big	loud	they
brother	matter	to
but	mother	too
can	no	tries
Danny	not	very
day	one	wants
far	play	where
father	roar	who
get	say	yes
he